ER
Nimmo, Jenny.

2-25-09

Matty mouse /

Matty Mouse

Crabtree Publishing Company
www.crabtreebooks.com

PMB 16A, 350 Fifth Avenue,
Suite 3308,
New York, NY 10118

616 Welland Avenue,
St. Catharines, Ontario
Canada, L2M 5V6

For George and Tom

J.N.

For Ami and Aden

R.R.

Cataloging-in-Publication data is available at the Library of Congress

Published by Crabtree Publishing in 2006
First published in 2003 by Egmont Books Ltd.
Text copyright © Jenny Nimmo 2003
Illustrations copyright © Ruth Rivers 2003
The Author and Illustrator have asserted their moral rights.
Paperback ISBN 0-7787-0898-5
Reinforced Hardcover Binding ISBN 0-7787-0852-7

1 2 3 4 5 6 7 8 9 0 Printed in Italy 5 4 3 2 1 0 9 8 7 6

Matty Mouse

Jenny Nimmo

Illustrated by Ruth Rivers

BLue Bananas

Matty Mouse had done it again.

He'd had another accident.

He'd filled the kitchen sink with water

and pretended it was a swimming pool.

The running tap made

a great waterfall.

When Matty went to get his plastic ducks, he forgot to turn off the tap. By the time his mom got to the sink it was too late.

Oh, Matty!

Sorry about the puddle, Mommy.

"Matty, you must think about what
you're doing," said Mrs. Mouse.
Matty said he would try really hard
to think about what he was doing,
but then he forgot, because he was
pretending to be a zombie.

Vroom!

The next day, when Matty came
in from playing, he was pretending
to be a jet. He zoomed into the
kitchen and left the front door open.

A cold draft whistled through
the house and shook
Mr. Mouse's newspaper.

"Shut the door, Matty!" he said.

"Why?" asked Matty.

"Why do you think?" asked his dad.

"I don't know," said Matty.

"Think!" said Mr. Mouse.

"It's time you put on your thinking cap," said his dad.

"Where is it?" asked Matty.

"Where do you think?" asked his dad.

Try and think, son.

I am thinking, Dad.

Matty went to his room to look

for a thinking cap.

He put all sorts of things on his head,

but none of them seemed to help.

He became an astronaut,

a dinosaur,

a chef,

a pop star,

and a ghost,

but he still didn't

know why he had to

shut the front door.

Rooaarr!

Ah, ha!

wooh!

"Poor Matty," said Mrs. Mouse. "We should tell him that no one can actually see a thinking cap."

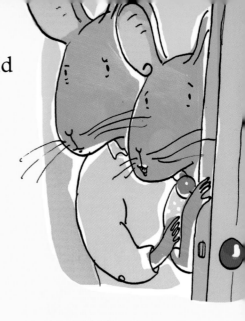

None of these are right.

"He must find out for himself," said Mr. Mouse. "After all, that's what a thinking cap is. It just means you have to think extra hard."

When Matty had tried on all
his hats, he decided to look
for a thinking cap outside.

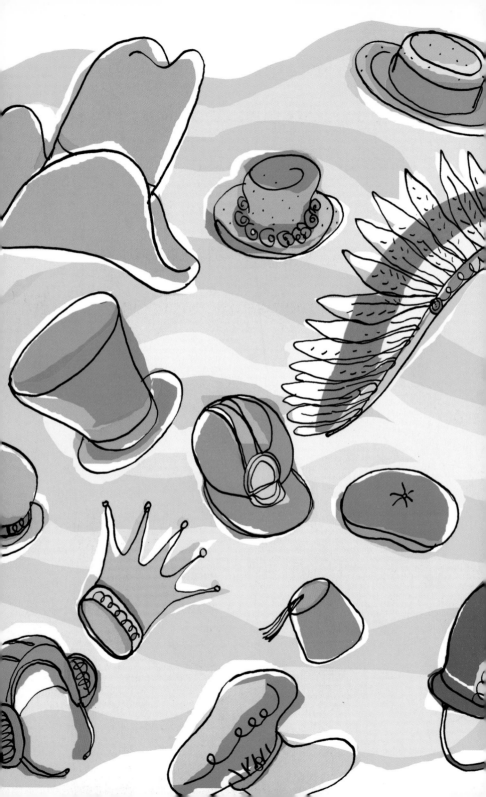

"Don't forget, we're going to have

lunch with Grandma!" shouted his dad.

"I won't," said Matty.

But he wasn't really listening.

He was too busy wondering what

color his thinking cap would be.

Matty ran into a field. He spotted an acorn cup. It looked just right. A squirrel was watching Matty from a high branch.

"Is this a thinking cap?" asked Matty.

"How should I know?"

asked the squirrel.

Matty put

the acorn cup on

his head. He closed his eyes

This feels perfect.

and thought about the front door.

The squirrel began to laugh. "You look

really funny," he said.

"This isn't my thinking cap," cried

Matty. "I still don't know

But it still doesn't work.

why I have to shut the

front door."

21

Matty took off the acorn cup and ran into a forest. On the forest floor he spied a flower head. It looked just right. "Maybe this is a thinking cap," he said.

What do you look like?

Tum-ti-tum

A bee watched Matty put the flower on his head. Matty peered at his reflection in a puddle. I look like an alien, he thought.

A big, scary, purple alien!

Just then, the bee began to buzz

around Matty's head. It chased him

out of the forest and

into the park. "Help!"

cried Matty.

Buzz, buzz, buzzz

Shoo, bee.

He pulled off the flower head and

flung it at the bee. "Leave me alone,

I'm only a mouse."

Matty took cover under a park bench.

He didn't see the old woman sewing,

or the old man sitting beside her.

All at once, something dropped out

of the sky and landed in front of

Matty. It was a beautiful silver hat.

"Oooo!" Matty said. "That has to be my thinking cap." He quickly pulled it over his head.

A voice above Matty said, "You've dropped your thimble, dear." Down came a big thumb and finger, and picked up the thimble with Matty's head still stuck inside.

Whoa! I'm stuck.

"Help!" squeaked Matty, dropping
from a great height. "Giants!"

He bounced on to the
path and ran and ran until
the park bench was out of sight.

"That silver hat was much too small for giants," he sighed. "They must have very tiny thoughts."

At that moment, Matty almost tripped over a baby's mitten.

Seems too large for a thinking cap, Matty said to himself, but perhaps I'll have large thoughts. At last, I'll find out why I must shut the front door.

Just as Matty pulled on the mitten, the baby's mother noticed that it was missing. She turned back and picked it up.

Goo-goo.

Silly me, your mitten.

29

Matty was still inside, but she didn't see him. She put the mitten beside the baby and pushed them both out of the park and into the supermarket.

What shall we get you for din-dins?

Ma ma ma ma.

Best Buy

Inside the mitten, Matty was getting very hot. "This can't be a thinking cap," he mumbled. "I can hardly breathe and I certainly can't think." He wriggled out of the mitten and jumped from the baby carriage.

Here goes!

"A mouse!" someone screamed.

Two boys chased Matty down the supermarket aisle, while customers screamed, carts collided, cans rolled everywhere, old ladies fell over, and bags flew in the air.

Matty had never been so frightened.

Where?

He rushed out of the supermarket, straight into a storm. Thunder growled, lightning flashed, and rain poured from the clouds. By the time Matty got home he was soaked.

Brrrrrrr.

"Mom! Mom!" called Matty. But his mom and dad were out. Where could they be?

Where is everyone?

Matty sat in a corner and tried to rub himself dry. But no matter how hard he rubbed, he just couldn't get warm. He'd forgotten to shut the door. He'd also forgotten about the visit to Grandma.

The wind whistled through the open door. The rain blew in. Garbage flew in. Paper, cans, twigs, and leaves littered the floor, and Matty got colder and colder.

"I wish I had a thinking cap," wailed

Matty, "then I'd know what to do."

Matty thought very hard.

Then he thought even harder.

Suddenly he had an idea.

Matty jumped up and shut the door.

SLAM!

Uck! It's all mucky.

He picked up all

the garbage.

He swept the floor and

dusted the furniture.

Nice and clean again.

In a few minutes, the house was

warm and dry. Then, feeling

very tired, Matty had

a little nap.

yaawwnn

When Matty's mom and dad came
home they found him fast asleep.

"Matty!" cried his mom, "where have
you been?"

Matty woke up with a start.

"We've been looking everywhere for
you," said Mrs. Mouse, giving Matty
a big hug. "We told you we were
going to lunch with Grandma Mouse.
When we couldn't find you, we
thought you must have climbed the
hill to Grandma's by yourself."

Mummy!
Daddy!

Matty told his mom and dad about the terrible things that had happened while he was searching for his thinking cap.

"I know why I must shut the door now," he said.

"If I don't, the wind and rain can come in, and all sorts of garbage."

"Matty, you've found your thinking cap," said Mr. Mouse.

"Have I?" he said.

"I can't see it."

"Thinking caps are invisible," said his dad, "but you can always tell when you've got one on. It means you're thinking properly."

"Oh, I see!" Matty tapped his head.

Look, Dad.

And then he saw a row of muddy
footprints leading from the door.
"Someone wasn't thinking about
wiping their feet when they came in,"
he said, giggling.

Who's not
got their thinking
cap on now?

"Oh dear!" Mr. Mouse looked down at his own muddy feet.

"Sometimes even dads can forget their thinking caps," laughed Mrs. Mouse.

"And before I forget, look what Grandma Mouse has sent you, Matty." She lifted a large chocolate cake out of her basket.

Yummy!

For you, Matty.

"Wow! I'm going to remember today forever," said Matty.

That night, when he fell asleep, Matty dreamed that he could really see his thinking cap. It was made of sparkling silver stars, and every star was a thought.

Night night!